By

Neighla Cain

THE HOUSE

A thought-provoking look at the reality, of living in a country as an immigrant.

ISBN: 978-1-5272-4669-0 (Paperback)

Front cover image by Book Printing UK.

Book inside design by David Amuno

First printing edition 2019.

Published by: Neighla Cain

THE HOUSE

The best homes are the ones we build from scratch

Is the house you live in, really your home?

By Neighla Cain

PREFACE

This book is a view of modern-day society in the western world.

It uses several analogies to get people thinking about the country they live in and the potential mindset of some of the people in power.

The house outlines the conventional strategy of climbing the corporate ladder to become a financial success and eventually financially free. But whilst using a strategy in a system that was never designed for everyone to begin with.

The short story aims to get the reader thinking about alternative ways to become a financial success, away from the conventional way we have been taught.

INTRODUCTION

It all started one Winter's evening. A friend and I sat in his front room talking about life. The curtains were drawn, the TV was off, and the conversation was underway.

We began to discuss our personal stories and I shared an observation from a documentary that I had seen on TV. The documentary discussed many ideas. One being that the opportunities and the perception of ethnic minorities, were different to those who were, or looked like, people of English descent. The documentary went into detail providing stories and statistics of people in the UK, to highlight the points being addressed.

It ended by showing, how these factors had an influence on education, employment opportunities and people's mindset in general.

I asked, "Why do you think we are we not taught about money and investing in school?" "Why are we mainly exposed to negative things when it comes to non-British history being taught?

We went on to discuss the education system. The media and what we are shown, the police, the government and others in power. We discussed history, diet, the healthcare system, and our present environment for hours and hours. As the conversation began to close, my friend looked at me and laughed.

"What is so funny? I asked?

He responded, *"Just think of this country like one big purpose-built house".*

From there, the story was born.

FOREWORD

Have you ever heard these questions before?

- Why are there not many people who look like me in the workplace?
- Why didn't I get the job when I was more qualified than the person who did?
- Why have they closed all the youth centres and after school clubs, in my part of town?
- Why don't we learn more about my country's history in the schools?
- Why have they reduced youth funding for lower-income groups?

Though some of the answers to these questions are obvious, the reasons why many of these things happen, is known as unconscious bias, and it all comes down to one simple statement:

"It's not your house!"

CHAPTERS

CHAPTER 1

THE FOUNDATION

In a small town, many years ago, was a gentleman named John Smith. John was a traditional man, with very strong values and very big dreams. One of his biggest goals in life was to have a big family and to make sure he could provide for them. He wanted to build them a big house. John knew that to do this, he would need to find himself a good wife.

A year or so went by and John met Sarah. Sarah was a person who also had strong traditional values and she encompassed many of the qualities that John wanted in a woman. It wasn't long before John proposed to Sarah and within a few months, the couple became Mr. and Mrs. Smith.

As the couple grew in their relationship, they both shared their goal of building their dream home. John had big dreams and Sarah was great at planning. They both had a similar vision for what they wanted to get out of life.

"John" – Sarah would ask

"What is your vision for the future?"

John: *"Sarah my beloved wife. I would like to build a big house and to start a family. I want to have many children and for those children to do the same. When we build this house, I want to ensure that our children and all their children, will always have somewhere to live."*

Sarah: *"How big do you want it to be John?"* Sarah asked

John: *"It will eventually be a mansion, Sarah! With many rooms, each for an individual purpose.*

I will have a big kitchen, to ensure the Smiths will always have the best-made meals. There will be a prayer room, where as a family we

will pray and thank God for our blessings. There will be a first aid room where the children can go to get medicine if they are ever sick. We will have an education room and library, where we will keep all our Smith treasures and the children can learn about the family's history. This will include information that can be passed down forever so that when we are gone, the Smith family history will live on. Finally, there will be a large basement with a safe, where we can save our money. This way, when the house gets full, we can use this money to build additional rooms."

Sarah: *"It sounds great John!"*

John *"One of the main things I want from the house Sarah, is for all of the Smiths to have somewhere to live. They can contribute to the house by maintaining the rooms, but most importantly, they will live in the house rent-free. They will never have to pay to live here and will always have somewhere to stay. The bigger the family gets,* *the larger the house will grow but there will always be more than enough space for everyone."*

Sarah was so excited. *"John this is such an amazing idea! When are we going to start building?"*

John: *"Well why don't we start planning today."*

So, John and Sarah started building their house and though it took a few years, the house looked great and was finally complete.

The house was a large detached house sitting on many acres of land. Throughout the house, there were many rooms just as John had visualised and each was decorated with attention to detail. There was a distinct feeling in the house which made the couple beam with pride and they knew this was the start of their legacy. John and Sarah were very pleased.

"Some people look for a beautiful place, others make a place beautiful."

CHAPTER 2

THE CHILDREN

Once the house was complete and a few years had gone by, John and Sarah decided it was time to start a family and began trying for a baby. Within the year, Sarah was pregnant and nine months later gave birth to their first son, Paul Smith.

John looked at his new-born with great happiness and pride:

"You are my first-born son and you will pass down the family history," **he said**, as he looked into Paul's eyes whilst holding him for the first time.

John spent a great deal of time with Paul as a child,

teaching him the foundations of how to be a Smith and moulding him just the way he wanted. He knew he wanted all his children to be raised in the same way and with the same core foundations.

Two years later, Sarah was pregnant again and gave birth to Claire Smith. The couple went on to have 5 more children over the years. 3 more boys and 2 more girls.

John's ultimate goal was to ensure the family values were passed down to his children and so throughout the children's upbringing, he would check they were taught all about the Smiths values when studying in the education room in the house.

John wanted to ensure that once, he and his wife had passed, the Smith's legacy and family values would still live on. John would regularly check in with the children to ensure they knew what they should know and that they were being taught effectively.

As Paul was the eldest, John was often hardest on him. For this reason, whilst Paul was growing up, John would regularly ask him questions to ensure that he understood the family values in detail.

John: *"Paul, I would like to talk to you"*

Paul: *"Yes Dad, what would you like to speak about?"*

John: *"Can you tell me what the Smith family values are?*

Paul: *"Yes Dad. Of course. You are always testing me."*

John: *"Ok, go on…"*

Paul: *"The main values are to 1. To ensure the history of the Smiths and our family values are passed down onto all the new Smiths even after we are gone. 2. To ensure we are educated to always know how to manage and grow the Smith's house and mainly 3. To ensure any relations of the Smiths will always have a job in the house and have somewhere to live rent-free."*

John: *"That's fantastic son, please make sure you pass these values down to your children and I will be checking with your other siblings to ensure that they understand the values too."*

Paul: *"Oh, dad! You know I will pass these down. I am very proud to be a Smith!"*

John: *"I'm glad to hear it son"*

"Each day of our lives, we make deposits into the banks of our children."

CHAPTER 3

FAMILY GROWTH

As the years went by, Paul, Claire, and the other siblings all got married and went on to have several children. John and Sarah eventually grew old and passed away, but the motto of the house continued because all the children had constantly been taught to follow the Smith's values and to pass these down to their children, all of which lived in the house.

Each sibling oversaw various rooms in the house and as their families grew, they kept extending the house.

All family members would follow the same pattern, which was to be educated to young adult age, choose an area in the house to specialise in, help it grow and then extend when needed. Once becoming adults, they would then live rent-free, get married, have children of their own and repeat the cycle.

The subjects taught in the education room were tailored depending upon which part of the house the children would want to look after and there were specific teachings around those areas. For example, the children who wanted to maintain the safe and money in the basement would focus on Maths, the children who wanted to teach and maintain the education room and library would focus on English and History and those who wanted to run various areas of the house would focus on Business studies. There were lots of subjects and varied popularity amongst the different jobs in the house. As the house grew, there were jobs that many of the Smiths wanted to do as well as others that very few wanted to do. There was eventually a hierarchy set up. This taught the children that they would need to work their way up to the best jobs before becoming rent-free but start with the less desirable jobs that no one wanted to do first. The children were not very happy about this, but it was something that had to be enforced.

Many generations had now lived in the house and the house was getting crowded. The Smiths continued to extend it. As the house continued to grow, the education room and library became a selection of schools attached to the house. The big kitchen became several restaurants attached to the house. The first aid room became the central hospital. The prayer room became a big church and the big basement with the safe became the Smiths first family bank.

They built shops, places to buy food, entertainment establishments and tons of rooms for people to live in.

The Smith household was looking spectacular and everyone was proud of its growth. The growth was a benefit to everyone as it created lots of opportunities for the Smiths to work, to grow and to be entertained. Every establishment that was build came from an extended family member of the Smith's and there was a Smith's value undertone in every piece of the extended house.

John Smith's original motto was alive. He wanted the Smiths to have the best of everything. He wanted them to have establishments that would benefit any Smith. If he was still alive, he would have been proud to see that although he was no longer there, the Smith's name was still very apparent, and the values were instilled in everything new that was built.

Families are like
branches on a tree.
We grow in
different directions
but our roots
remain as one.

CHAPTER 4

THE SKIMS

As the house continued to grow, Paul, Claire, and their siblings, soon realised that they needed some help running the house. Claire wanted to hire some help from outside of the house, but Paul was not too keen.

Claire: *"Paul, this house is getting too big. We are going to need some help running it"*

Paul: *"I think we will be fine running the house by ourselves Claire."*

Claire: *"We can't do it all on our own Paul, let's hire some staff from international houses. The house has become too large for us to manage alone"*

Paul: *"I'm not sure Dad would have wanted that Claire. He built this house for the Smiths"*

Claire: *"Dad would prefer for us to get help rather than to see the house fail Paul. We need to do this for him. The workers will live here so they will still be taught the Smith values. That's what Dad mainly wanted.*

Paul: *"I don't agree. Look at our family values, Claire. How exactly can anyone who isn't a Smith fit into them?"*

Claire: *"Think about it, Paul. Dad's values were: To ensure the history of the Smiths and our family values are passed down onto all the new Smiths even after we are gone. Well, the workers will live in this house and learn about the Smiths history in school, so they will naturally pass these down automatically as they won't be taught anything else."*

Paul: *"Ok, I see what you mean and that is true. But what about the other family values?"*

Claire: *"The second value was to ensure we are educated to always know how to manage and grow the Smith's house. Well, Paul, they will be working in the Smith house so of course they will be growing it. They don't need to be taught about the management side. Us Smiths can continue to do that."*

Paul: *"I suppose if they live here in the house then you are right again. They will be growing it. The main value though Claire, how will we get around that one?"*

Claire: *"Paul, that one is simple. The value is to ensure that any relations of the Smiths will always have a job in the house and to have somewhere to live rent-free. Well, anyone who isn't a Smith will just pay rent! We will give them jobs but more of the ones that we don't want to do so that the Smiths can focus on running and* *building the bigger parts of the house. This will motivate the children as none of them want to do the less desirable jobs. You know this is true"*

Paul had a thoughtful look on his face.

Paul: *"Do you really think people will go for this though Claire?"*

Claire: *"Lots of people want to work in our house Paul so I think they will. Once they have a job in the house which is enough to cover the rent and maintain themselves, they will be happy."*

Paul: *"Ok, you do have a point Claire and I guess you are right. Let's do it."*

So, they began to hire some additional people to help manage the house. These people were from other houses, mainly international houses who were intrigued about the Smith's house and what happened inside there.

The Smiths had built up a good reputation and many were happy to work in their house as it was one of the biggest houses around.

Paul and Claire hired cooks, cleaners, gardeners, designers, doctors, nurses, teachers, bank clerks, and many more creating lots of jobs and helping many people from outside of the Smith's original family. They often reserved many of the better jobs for the Smiths although there was still a fair few people from outside of the Smiths extended family who had good jobs too.

Many of these workers went on to have children and their children also went on to have children too. All the workers and their children lived in the house. To differentiate between the Smiths and those from other houses, the nickname 'Skims' was quickly adopted. A Skim was either someone who was originally from another house or the child of someone who was from another house. This term was known by all.

There was a nurse who had lived in the house for a long time by the name of Veronica. She was the same age as Claire, John and Sarah's first daughter and had been working in the house since Claire had become an adult. She now worked at the hospital attached to the house.

She had a child named Shereen who had studied at the local school. Claire also had a child called Annabel, born around the same time. Annabel studied in the same class as Shereen.

Although Veronica had lived in another house before working in the Smith's hospital, Shereen had never lived or studied anywhere else. This house was all she knew. Shereen quickly saw from a young age that there were many opportunities for jobs she could do in and around the house and she knew she wanted one of the better jobs.

Shereen had only ever lived in this house and because she liked and respected how the house was run, her main aspiration was always to stay in the house, do well in her studies and work her way up to where Annabel was.

Annabel was her best friend and although they had finished school at the same time, she was only in her early 20's yet was already living in the house rent-free.

Alone we can
do so little,
together
we can do so
much more.

CHAPTER 5

WHEN THE PENNY DROPPED

One day Shereen decided to enquire about how Annabel had managed to be living rent-free so quickly. She had this same aspiration and figured if Annabel had done it, she could just follow the same strategy. As far as she knew, they had gone to the same school and had the same education. Annabel was also her best friend and had always been very open and honest with her throughout their years at school. Shereen waited for the right moment and then decided to have a talk with Annabel.

Shereen: *"Hey Annabel, how are you?"*

Annabel: *"I'm good Shereen and you?"*

Shereen: *"I'm good but wanted to ask you something?"*

Annabel: *"Of course Shereen, you know I tell you everything"*

Shereen: *"You do, and I trust you a lot. I just wanted to know, how come you are already living in the house rent-free? We went to school together and have done similar jobs, so I'm not totally sure what we have done differently. Not many people our age seem to be rent-free, but I would like to be rent-free too."*

Annabel: *"Well to be honest Shereen, and not a lot of people know this, but it is because my grandparents were the ones who built this house. When they built it, one of the family values that my Grandad created was that anyone who is a Smith will be able to live in the house rent-free once they reach adult age."*

Shereen: *"Oh I see, I truly wasn't aware. Thank you for letting me know that Annabel"*

Annabel: *"No problem, but can I ask you not to tell too many people. I don't want people to think I've not worked hard because we both know I have"*

Shereen: *"Yeah, that's fine Annabel. You can trust me"*

"So, what about the Skims? Do you know if we will ever get to live rent-free?"

Annabel: *"To be honest Shereen, when the house was built, it wasn't built with the Skims in mind which is why you pay rent. My Grandad didn't know that you would be in the house. The house and the buildings attached to the house were only created with the Smiths in mind. I know that there are some Skims who are also living rent-free but when you are a Smith, it was in my Grandads plan that living rent-free would happen automatically."*

"Once you work hard, I know you can be rent-free too though. You are a hard worker Shereen, so you will be able to get to the rent-free status for sure"

Shereen: *"Ok, I appreciate the compliment Annabel and thank you for being honest. I have a better understanding now"*

Shereen felt a little saddened about some of the things that Annabel had shared. Her mum, Veronica had been in the house for many years. The same amount of time as Claire, Annabel's mum. Veronica, however, was still paying rent despite working at least 20 years longer. It now started to make sense why.

Shereen was a very driven and determined character and decided that she was not going to be like her mum paying rent for so many years.

"Mum probably didn't apply herself properly when she was younger," **She thought.**

Shereen wanted to live rent-free. Yes, Annabel had a head start but she believed if Annabel could do it, so could she.

She set herself a goal that within 5 years she wanted to have one of the best jobs in the house and to eventually be living rent-free. She wanted to see which other Skims had achieved this and how they did it so that she could follow the same path.

Living rent-free meant a lot to Shereen. She could immediately see the differences in her and Annabel's lifestyles due to Annabel having rent free status.

Annabel had time. Time to do what she wanted to do and pursue her passions rather than spending all her hours working. When she did work, it was more to learn new skills and was by choice rather than working to only pay rent and bills like most other people were doing.

She had more money. Annabel had no rent to pay, so any money she made went into her pocket. She was able to live the lifestyle she wanted to due to this. She travelled regularly, bought whatever she wanted and spend a lot of time investing both in the house to further grow it and investing into her younger relatives and extensions of their family to ensure they followed a similar path. Shereen knew this was something she also wanted to do.

The strategy based on what she had learned at school seemed pretty simple she thought:

Step 1: Go to school to get educated.

Step 2: Find a job in the house (any job) to gain work experience whilst trying to work her way up to a better job.

There could be some additional studying required in the process if it was a particular area of the house that she wanted to work in.

Step 3: Get one of the best jobs in the house and work there.

Step 4: After working there for a while, become rent-free.

Shereen also knew that even if you never became rent-free, after you had been working somewhere for many years, you were entitled to half price rent. This didn't sound too bad but Shereen was still determined that she would reach rent-free status.

Her next step was to do some research on how to do it.

"Education is learning what you didn't know, you didn't know."

George Boaz

CHAPTER 6

THE VISITS

Shereen decided to visit some of the different parts of the extended house to do some research on the people who were working and to see how many people were living rent-free. Her main aim was to find out how they did it, especially if they were Skims. Some of the things that Annabel said were also playing on her mind. In particular, that her Grandad didn't know the Skims would have ever been in the house.

She decided to start with the school where she and Annabel used to study and see some of her old teachers. She saw 3 of her teachers Mrs. Williams, Mr. Patel and Mrs. Horowitz. She believed they were all Skims based on their appearance.

Shereen: *Hi Miss, Sir, do you mind if I ask you a few questions about my career development?*

Mrs. Williams: *"Hey Shereen, how are you? No of course not, what would you like to know?"*

Shereen: *"Well, I would like to live in this house rent-free, so I am just trying to get ideas from other people who are Skims that may already be living rent-free. You all have good jobs. Are any of you teachers currently living rent-free in the house?"*

All teachers: *"No Shereen, none of us are living rent-free just yet, it will take a few more years at least"*

Shereen: *"Oh ok, thank you. Can I ask another question?"*

Mr. Patel: *"Yes Shereen, you can."*

Shereen: *"Do all of your children come to this school?"*

All teachers: *"Yes, all of our children come or have come to this school Shereen."*

Shereen: *"Ok my last question: Who decides what you teach your children in this school? As in, the main Syllabus?"*

Mrs. Horowitz: *"The Syllabus was written many years ago and I believe that the Smiths who originally built the house, decide what content we teach the children. They have always wanted all who study here to understand the history of the Smiths and how to look after this house"*

Shereen: *"Do you ever teach anything different?"*

Mrs. Williams: *"No Shereen, when we became teachers, we were given strict guidelines not to move away from the main syllabus"*

Shereen: *"Ok thank you."*

Shereen left the school feeling thoughtful. None of the Skims working in the school were living rent-free and everyone was being taught how to live in a house that in the first instant was only built to educate the Smiths with little change to the syllabus. Shereen decided to go to a few more places around the house on her mission to find some Skims living rent-free.

The next stop was the local hospital that was attached to the house. She decided to see her doctor, Mr. Chow.

She asked him the same questions.

Shereen: *"Hey doc, how are you?*

Mr. Chow: *"Hi Shereen, good to see you."*

Shereen: *"Do you mind if I ask you a few questions about my career development?"*

Mr. Chow: *"No of course not Shereen, what would you like to know?"*

Shereen: *"Well, I would like to live in this house rent-free, so I am just trying to get ideas from other people who are Skims that may already be living rent-free. You have a good job. Are any of your doctors or nurses currently living rent-free in the house?"*

Mr. Chow: *"No Shereen, none of us are living rent-free just yet, it will take a few more years at least."*

Shereen: *"Oh ok, thank you. Can I ask another question?"*

Mr. Chow: Yes Shereen, you can.

Shereen: *"Do all of your children get treated in this hospital?"*

Mr. Chow: *"Yes, our children come here if they are sick although I must say sometimes my wife's home remedies work better than the medicine."*

Shereen: *"Ok my last question, who decides what medicine is used in this hospital and who has it been tested on?"*

Mr. Chow: *"The Smiths who originally built the house decide what medicine we use in the hospital. They have always worked well for generations when the Smiths have been sick."*

Shereen: *"Ok thank you."*

The next place that Shereen went to, was the biggest restaurant attached to the house. There she saw one of her favourite chefs, Mrs. Mensah and asked her the same questions about all the chefs and the restaurant staff.

Shereen: *"Mrs. Mensah, do you mind if I ask you a few questions about my career development?"*

Mrs. Mensah: *"Oh, would you like to be a chef Shereen?"*

Shereen: *"Well, not exactly, Mrs. Mensah. I would like to live in this house rent-free, so I am just trying to get ideas from other people who are Skims who may already be living rent-free. Are any of your cooks currently living rent-free in the house?"*

Mrs. Mensah: *"No Shereen, none of us are living rent-free just yet, it will take a few more years at least."*

Shereen: *"Oh ok, thank you. Can I ask another question?"*

Mrs. Mensah: *"Yes Shereen, you can."*

Shereen: *"Do all of your children eat the food that you cook?"*

Mrs. Mensah: *"Yes, they eat the food that we provide to the school, but I also cook special recipes for my children when I make their evening meals. These dishes seem to help them develop and grow better"*

Shereen: *"Ok my last question: who decides what food you give to the children in the school Miss?*

Mrs. Mensah: *"The recipes were decided many years ago and I believe the Smiths who originally built the house decide what food we give the children. They have always wanted the best food for the Smiths."*

Shereen: *"Oh ok thank you."*

Shereen was building a picture but decided to go to one last place to be certain.

The Smiths family bank was behind the house. She knew her Uncle Nelson worked there and that he would be open and honest with her about everything he knew. He was a senior member of staff in the bank, so she knew he must know at least 1 skim who lived rent-free.

She walked into the bank and almost immediately saw her Uncle.

Shereen: *"Hey uncle, how are you?!"*

Uncle Nelson: *"Shereen, long time! How are you and how is your mum?"*

Shereen: *"Yes, everyone is well. Uncle, I need you to help me with something. Is it me or are most of the businesses attached to the house, mainly here to serve the Smiths and their extended family? They seem to be the only people I have come across living rent-free. I've gone everywhere!"*

Uncle Nelson: *"No Shereen, that isn't the case and I don't want you to think that way. We help many Skims here in the bank. We are always lending out money to help people and its especially important for the Skims as it assists them in paying their rent."*

"Yes, there have been a few Skims with financial difficulty, but we continue to lend them money here in the bank to help them. We just add a little interest to keep the bank running"

Shereen: *"Ok so the bank borrows money with interest to the Skims. Then the Skims use it to pay rent to the Smiths. Is that correct?"*

Uncle Nelson: *"You say it like it's a bad thing Shereen. Look at the house we live in, look at the shops we can spend our money in. The bank is very helpful Shereen. It ensures we can continue to afford to spend what we want as well as getting our rent paid."*

Shereen: *"Ok I see where you are coming from Uncle but if the Skims keep getting into debt, how will they ever save their money or even build their own houses one day?"*

Uncle Nelson: *"Build houses? Shereen we live in this house. Most of us live very well in this house- why go through all the trouble of building our own?" Yes, we pay rent, but we get a lot of benefits. We have it much better than your grandparents did when they first moved to this house"*

"Shereen love, all you need to do is work hard and get one of the top jobs in the house so that you don't have to pay rent and then you will be laughing. You will have it all!"

Shereen: *"But uncle, I have hardly come across any Skims who don't pay rent!"*

Uncle Nelson: *"Shereen, my Godson Anthony doesn't pay rent, so I know it is possible."*

Shereen: *"Oh wow, Anthony doesn't pay rent? Where can I find him?"*

Uncle Nelson: *"He works at the TV studio at the back of the house."*

Shereen: *"Ok uncle, thank you, speak to you soon."*

Shereen left a little frustrated.

Within a week, she had spoken to hundreds of people, about hundreds of people and there was still only a very small portion of Skims living rent-free in comparison to the Smiths and extended families of the Smiths. What frustrated her more, was the number of people who didn't mind and thought that it was better to live in a house that was not built for them whilst paying rent than to leave the house and try and live somewhere else rent-free. There were also many Skims holding onto the fact that if they kept doing exactly what they were doing, one day they would also be rent-free. Although Shereen wanted to believe that this could be true as she once did, her mum, Uncle Nelson, Mrs. Williams, Mr. Patel, and Mr. Chow were just a few examples of people she had seen working hard for most of her life who were still not rent-free. Maybe the process taught to everyone in the Smith school wasn't a strategy that worked for everyone. Anthony was one of the first people Shereen had found who was a similar age to her that didn't pay rent.

Shereen continued to think:

The school's curriculum was not made for the Skims but was made for the Smiths.

The food and medicine were not the best for the Skims but are the best for the Smiths.

The banks keep the Skims in debt, so they rely on their jobs. This keeps the Skims paying rent and as the Skims spend in their shops, the Smith household continues to grow.

Shereen started to feel a little upset again.

Yes, she loved the house, she loved her friends including Annabel, but something seemed unfair. Her mum was working for as long as she could remember and was still paying rent. Her Grandmother was still paying rent until the day she died. How easy was it to become rent-free in a house that was not designed for the Skims in the first place? There must be another way.

"Truth is available only to those who have the courage to question what they have been taught."

CHAPTER 7

THE SHOPPING TRIP

It was the day of the annual sale. This was a great day for all as it allowed the Smith residents to buy anything they wanted in the house at a discounted price. Shereen and her family would often spend hours shopping, eating and purchasing things from the different shops in the house. Shereen would always look forward to the annual sale day but today, she felt slightly different.

"So much extra money is now being spent, building the Smiths house and mainly by the Skims." **she thought.**

Nevertheless, there were a few things she needed, and she decided to contact Annabel to come to the shops with her.

Shereen: *"Annabel, are you free to come shopping today?"*

Annabel: *"Yes sure Shereen, I don't really like shopping as much as I used to, but I am more than happy to come with you to buy some things"*

Shereen: *"How come you don't really like shopping that much anymore?"* **Shereen asked intrigued.**

Ever since Annabel had told Shereen about her family legacy, Shereen would always be interested in the actions of Annabel and why she did or didn't do things. This was never something she would pay attention to before, but she now knew that understanding more about Annabel would be important on her journey to becoming rent-free.

Annabel: *"Don't get me wrong Shereen, I enjoy having new items, but my Grandad always taught us to only buy things that will help to grow the house, investments. When I go shopping in these sales,*

I am always tempted to buy things I don't need and spend more than I planned. I suppose if money is being spent in the shops that are a part of the house, it is in some way growing the house anyway", **she said thoughtfully.** *"Ok, I'll be ready in an hour".*

So Shereen and Annabel hit the shops. For the first time, Shereen had viewed the shopping trip with a fresh pair of eyes, analysing everything around her. The first thing she realised was the excitement of so many people and especially the Skims, who were almost desperately spending money in the shops. People were so happy to spend in these shops, although based on what Uncle Nelson had said previously, many people were borrowing money to do so.

She thought, *"Even for those who can afford it, these purchases only benefit the growth of the Smiths house and nothing else"*. She knew she had also been one of these people in the past.

"Why did I use to spend so much, **she thought** *and why wasn't I taught to invest like Annabel was?"*

She quickly realised, that when she used to spend recklessly, it was often fuelled by emotion.

In the past, her biggest aspiration was to work her way to the top of the Smith household and to live rent-free. She knew on some level, spending in these shops, buying clothing from these shops and doing the things that rent-free people did, made her feel like she was closer to that. She just kept thinking that the reality of it was, that this spending was taking her further away from creating anything of her own. In addition to the fact that if she wasn't rent-free, then trying to look like she was, was even more ridiculous.

As Shereen and Annabel continued through the shops, for the first time Shereen felt less excited about spending than she ever had before. Annabel wanted to buy some new shoes and so together they went into one of the high-end shoe shops. They both found something they liked and went over to the till.

On checkout, the cashier stared intensely at Annabel for several seconds and then eventually asked: *"Miss, do you have a Privilege card?"*

Annabel: *"Oh yes, I do actually"*

Annabel rummaged through her bag and went on to hand her Privilege card to the cashier. He then took a further discount off her purchase. When they left the shop, Shereen wanted to know more.

Shereen: *"Annabel, what is a Privilege Card and how do I get one?"*

Annabel: *"Oh, it's another thing my Grandad started Shereen. It's the Smiths Privilege card. When we buy things in the house, we get discounts. It also entitles us to live rent-free, it helps us on applications when we are applying for jobs and it comes in handy in so many ways. Even when we get into trouble!"*

Shereen: *"So I'm guessing the Skims wouldn't be able to get one of these cards?"* **Shereen said doubtfully**

Annabel: *"Unfortunately not Shereen. I know it's a bit unfair. I didn't even ask to have this Privilege card and I wish you could have one too, but because I'm a Smith, it's just the way it is."*

Shereen took a long sigh: *"Yeah, it's fine, I understand."*

As Shereen and Annabel were leaving the shops, Shereen bumped into her uncle Nelson, looking very pleased with himself in a brand-new luxury car.

Uncle Nelson: *"Hey Shereen, look what I just bought?"*

Shereen: *"Nice car uncle. I bet that set you back a bit"*

Uncle Nelson: *"Well I was saving for a while but then borrowed a bit from the bank to cover the rest. My colleague Peter had a similar one and I thought it could be my treat for working in the bank for so long. I'm almost near retirement age now"*

Shereen: *"Ok nice, you are retiring soon? So, are you living rent-free now uncle?"*

Uncle Nelson: *"No Shereen, not everyone gets there but I may as well enjoy myself whilst I'm here. I will also be entitled to half price rent once I retire which I'm looking forward to!"*

Shereen: *"Ok uncle, well enjoy. You will have to take us for a spin one day"*

Shereen felt annoyed at her uncle but just knew there was no point in even attempting to explain to him why. There were so many reasons.

The first being that he had saved his money, to simply put it right back into a major purchase which would grow the Smiths house and still give him nothing in return away from a material good. It wouldn't get him closer to living rent-free, building something of his own or anything that could have a lasting benefit.

The second reason being, how happy he was for the purchase. It was almost like the car had given him a sense of status that he didn't actually have.

The third reason being, that he had to borrow some of the money from the bank to get the car, meaning he could not afford it and was again indebted to the Smiths house. The fourth reason was, he was almost retired. He had worked in the bank almost his whole life and all he would have to show for it at the end was a luxury car and a car loan debt. Nothing to pass down to the children, no closer to living rent-free, no strategy for his children to live rent-free but immediate gratification from his behalf. She knew so many Skims lived like this and she felt even more determined to do something differently.

"Rich people stay rich by living like they are broke. Broke people stay broke by living like they are rich."

"It is easier to build strong children than to repair broken men."

CHAPTER 8

BACK TO SCHOOL

Shereen decided to go back to the school to see if any of the teachers knew why so many Skims were still paying rent. She had a lot of respect for Mrs. Williams. She was very intelligent and had helped her a lot during her school years. The other teachers were also very smart and were bound to give her some insight.

When she got to the school, to her surprise Mr. Patel and Mrs. Horowitz were no longer there.

Shereen: *"Hey Mrs. Williams, where have the other two teachers gone?"*

Mrs. Williams: *"Oh Mrs. Horowitz and Mr. Patel have left. They were only working here temporarily to save some money. They have decided to build their own houses with their families and work in a school they will build there." So, there will be at least two other houses now.*

Shereen: *"Oh wow, how cool. Tell me more."*

Mrs. Williams: "I don't know too much other than they have decided to build their own schools and teach their own syllabus so that they can learn about their own history instead of only that of the Smiths.

Shereen: *"That sounds like a really good idea!* ***Said Shereen****. "So, Mrs. Williams, why didn't you go and build your own house too?"*

Mrs. Williams: *"They have no idea how long it will take to build their houses. It could be many years Shereen. When they build the house, it will take a while before it is anywhere near the size of this* *house. I may not even be alive by the time their houses are at the level of this one.*

I decided to stay here. I'm sure if I continue to work hard, one day I'm going to live rent-free."

Shereen: *"What about your children and their children?"* ***asked Shereen***. *"If you started building your house now, surely, they would be alive to see the new house, have places to work and live rent-free forever?"*

Mrs. Williams: *"Possibly, but there's no guarantee. I'd prefer to just take my chances here and try to work my way up. I'm happy here"*

Shereen felt a little confused. Mrs. Williams had a point. This was a really nice house. Shereen had been there her whole life and had been reaping a lot of the great benefits.

But then she thought of the odds of the other people in the house. There were Skims who were even older than Annabel and Shereen, even older than her mum and still with no prospects of ever living rent-free.

Shereen thought: *"If I live rent-free in this house, my children will still need to work through the house as hard as I did, whereas if I build my own house, it would be a guarantee that they wouldn't have to pay rent. She would set up a rule just like Annabel's grandparents did. This would give them a helping hand."*

Shereen quickly knew, the smartest thing to do would be to build her own house. *"If Mr. Patel and Mrs. Horowitz could build, then so can I"*, ***she thought.***

She decided to pay them both a visit.

"The difference between the impossible and the possible lies within a mans determination."

Tommy Lasorda

CHAPTER 9

THE PATEL HOUSE:

After travelling for a while, Shereen finally arrived at the Patel house. It was very apparent to her that it was the Patel house from the moment she arrived. The house was different from that of the Smiths. Many people in the house looked like Mr. Patel although, like the Smiths household, several people looked a little different too.

Shereen knocked on the door and was pleasantly surprised when her former teacher Mr. Patel answered the door.

Mr. Patel: *"Shereen, how are you and what are you doing here?*

Shereen: *"Hi Sir, Mrs. Williams told me that you had built your own house and I thought it was an amazing idea. I just had to see it!"*

Mr. Patel: *"Well yes, I'm glad you are here Shereen. Thank you for coming to see us. As you can see, we still have some work to do to get our house as big as the Smiths household, but I am really happy with the progress we have made so far"*

Shereen: *"Yeah, I think it is admirable that you have even got started, Sir. What made you want to build your own house?"*

Mr. Patel: *"There were a few reasons Shereen. I'll explain them to you.*

The first reason was that since moving to the Smiths house, I felt as though everything I was doing was benefitting their house and I felt as though, if I didn't build my own, my children, their children and generations to come, would be doing the same. I wanted to change the cycle."

Shereen listened intently. This was exactly how she was feeling after doing all her visits.

Shereen: *"What were the other reasons, Sir?"* **She asked**

Mr. Patel: *"Shereen, I would have been paying rent in the Smiths house for good if I didn't build my own. I want to be rent-free and provide that platform for anyone who wants to build with me. I can do that much easier here."*

Shereen: *"Yes, I see what you mean Mr. Patel,* **Shereen said.** *"Were there any other reasons?"*

Mr. Patel: *"Shereen, before I got to the Smith house many years ago, and whilst my parents were still alive, I lived elsewhere. When I lived there, I learned a lot about where I was from and more things which specifically benefitted me and those like me. But I feel like* *since I've lived in the Smiths house, all I learned about is what is best for the Smiths and when anything about my previous house is mentioned, the information is often bias or inaccurate. In my new house, I can teach people who live here about more than just the Smiths way. I have the control to choose what I can and can't do here whereas I was limited when I lived in the other house. Does this all make sense Shereen?"*

Shereen: *"It makes perfect sense to me Mr. Patel. Thank you for sharing"*

Mr. Patel: *"No problem Shereen. Let me show you around some of the rooms in the house?"*

Shereen: *"Yes, please!"*

Mr. Patel proceeded to show Shereen around the different rooms in the house. Like the Smith's original house, there was an education room and library, a big kitchen, a prayer room and a lot of small corner shops. They all looked and felt different from the Smith's house, but it was clear the foundations were the same. Although it was a lot smaller than the Smith house, Shereen knew that one day this was going to be a big amazing place and Mr. Patel had started it from scratch. Whilst walking around she looked at the other people working in the house, the family members of the Patel's and extended family that were in the house. She immediately noticed the sense of pride each of the people working there had. She hadn't seen this look for a while when being in the Smiths house. Though many were happy working there, there was something different about the Patel house and she assumed it may be the fact that everyone knew they were working together for a bigger cause. Shereen felt inspired.

Shereen: *"Mr. Patel, thank you for showing me around and introducing me to your family. I noticed your son is not here though. Does he live here too?"*

Mr. Patel: *"That's a good question Shereen. My son Amit is just a bit older than you and was born in the Smiths house. When I told him, I was building the house, although he was happy about it, he didn't want to leave."*

Shereen: *"Oh wow, as much as that is unfortunate for you, I can understand why it is a hard decision to leave the Smith house as many people I have come across have felt the same"*

Mr. Patel: *"Yes originally I was a bit upset but he explained to me, he doesn't need to live here to build the house which I now see is the truth"*

Shereen: *"I don't understand Mr. Patel. What do you mean?"*

Mr. Patel: *"Well its simple Shereen. Amit continues to work and live in the Smiths house, but when it comes to any purchases he makes, professionals he deals with, the food he eats, places he prays, businesses he invests in, he does that in the Patel house. So away from his rent, everything he does is still growing the Patel house. He will ensure this is the strategy he passes down to his children if he chooses to permanently live here."*

Shereen: *"Oh so he has the best of both worlds?*

Mr. Patel: *"Absolutely Shereen. He also now has two options for his children, which will both benefit the Patel house. Either work in our house or just ensure they put money back into our house if they don't live here and choose to live elsewhere."*

Shereen: *"That sounds smart sir. I have seen enough and love what you have done here."*

Mr. Patel: *"No problem Shereen. I am glad to have been of assistance. Safe travels."*

"Oh, and Shereen. Please know you can come here to shop anytime. We have many great women's beauty stores here. Our range of hair products are the best". **Mr. Patel said smiling**

Shereen: *"Ok thank you for that Sir. There doesn't seem to be many other shops of this kind where I live so I might be back."*

Shereen left Mr. Patel's house feeling inspired. She realized that he had the same outlook on the Smiths household as she did. She wanted to speak with Mrs. Horowitz to see if her house was similar or different from Mr. Patel's and went on a journey to find it.

"No one ever made a difference by being like everyone else."

P.T Barnum

CHAPTER 10

THE HOROWITZ HOUSE

Later that afternoon, Shereen went on to visit Mrs. Horowitz in her new house. The Horowitz household was bigger than the Patel's at first glance with a lot going on. Shereen knocked on the door and Mrs. Horowitz answered.

Mrs. Horowitz: *"Shereen, how are you?"*

Shereen: *"I'm good miss. I have just come from Mr. Patel's house and was really intrigued to see yours. Can you tell me about it?"*

Mrs. Horowitz: *"Yeah sure Shereen. Well, the Horowitz house was built for my family and any extended family members. We have very strong values here. We buy, eat, pray, shop and educate our children, all in this house. Before we think of leaving this house to visit any* *other house, we would have exhausted every possible option here. We want to keep everything in this house if we can"*

Shereen: *"Ok, but don't you miss the Smiths house and the variety and choice of things they had."*

Mrs. Horowitz: *"I did a little in the beginning, but because everyone here is working to grow this house, it is growing at a much faster pace. We live very simply here. No flashy clothes, cars or jewellery. Everything we need is here and an extended family member can provide it. It keeps everyone happy, feeling as though they are contributing to the growth of the house and most importantly, it makes everyone wealthier. No one pays rent here Shereen! I still get to teach in our education room but I'm teaching topics that will benefit the residents in the house, not just the Smith Syllabus."*

Shereen: *"Ok I understand. Well done Miss. It looks amazing here. I've seen enough. Thank you."*

Shereen left feeling excited and was thankful to have been able to see the other houses. *"I can do this!"* **She thought.**

"I will work my way to the top of the Smith house as planned to maximise my earning potential, save and invest to make more money on the way and then I'm going to use that money to build my own house."

She was determined, motivated and unstoppable.

"The things you do
for yourself are
gone when you are
gone but the things
you do for others
remain your legacy."

Kalu Kalu

CHAPTER 11

THE VISIT TO ANTHONY

Shereen knew she needed help. She knew if other Skims helped her, she could build this house so much faster than if she did it alone. She knew she had to see Anthony. He was living rent-free, so he would have the time and money to help build the house for sure. Shereen takes a trip to the TV studio where she finds Anthony.

Shereen: *"Hey Ant, how are you?"*

Anthony: *"Hey Shereen, oh I'm great, living the dream man. What are you doing here?"*

Shereen: *"I've got a great idea, Anthony. Why don't we build our own house?"*

Anthony looked at Shereen blankly.

Anthony: *"Why would I want to do that Shereen?"*

Shereen: *"So, that you will be able to live rent-free Ant."*

Anthony: *"Ok that's nice but I live rent-free here already Shereen. It would take us ages to build a house as nice as this one."*

Shereen- *"Yeah, I understand that, but you are the only person I know living rent-free, whose parents were Skims. What about everyone else, what about your kids? I've learned recently that everything here was not built for you. It wasn't designed to have you or your children's best interest at heart."*

Anthony: *"Shereen it's nice what you are trying to do but honestly, I'm rent-free, my kids will be rent-free and I'm going to teach them how to work their way to the top of the house, so their kids are rent-free too."*

"Besides my wife is a Smith and she won't want to move."

Shereen: *"I'm not even asking you to move you know Anthony, just to help me to build. That way your kids and everyone else's kids will have more options when they grow up"*

Anthony: *"There are plenty of options here, Shereen. I know quite a few other people whose parents were Skims and they are living rent-free.*

"I can relate to what you are saying about the house not having my best interest at heart, all of the time. Sometimes they air things at the TV station which seem very bias towards the Smiths and against the Skims, but I believe all the best things are here in this house and I'm fine with living here forever. I would do the same if I was you. You are doing well, and I know you will also be rent-free in no time Shereen."

Shereen: *"How exactly did you become rent-free out of curiosity Anthony?"*

Anthony: "From a young age, I was always very confident and loved to talk so my parents put me into an additional school to help develop my talent alongside the Smith school. There was a lot of studying when I was younger Shereen and very little time for play. But in the end, I was able to secure a job in presenting. I met my Mrs in the school, and it opened a lot of doors for me. It exposed me to a lot of things, people and a strategy I may have never been taught if I followed the conventional school system. Now that I'm rent-free, I just do my presenting now and again whilst enjoying my life with my wife and kids"

Shereen: "That's great Anthony. So, it sounds like developing your natural talent helped you, along with additional education separate from the Smith's school system. Have you shared what you did with any other Skims?

Anthony: *Shereen, it may sound harsh, but I don't really care about everyone else. They should have just worked hard like me. I can't carry everyone. Once my family is fine, that is my biggest priority"*

Shereen: *"Ok Anthony, I understand"*

Shereen could see Anthony wasn't interested. It was sad that he could only see how the house had helped him but couldn't see the bigger picture and the importance of having a house of his own. The reason people loved and respected the house must have had something to do with the school system constantly giving a biased view of how great the Smith household was with nothing to compare it to. Many people probably never took a moment to think about this twice.

Shereen was still adamant to continue and made up her mind to build her own house regardless.

She decided to stay working in the Smith house with the plan that she was going to build her own house as soon as she saved enough. She wanted as many of the Skims to have the same plan.

She thought: *"All I need to do is explain to everyone that we can all live rent-free in the new house. It will eventually help everyone although it will take a while to build."*

She decided she would try to convince as many people of this as she could.

She went back to see Mrs. Williams in the school to try and convince her to assist in building the house. Mrs. Williams was not interested.

She went to see some of Mrs. Williams' children who said they will stay in the Smith house with their mum. She went to see many other Skims. They all decided they were happier working and living in the Smiths house for good. Shereen realised that after years of being educated in a house which told you how great they were, the fear of the unknown was likely overwhelming for people. No one would want to leave without understanding the bigger picture and she was only fortunate enough to know the bigger picture because Annabel trusted her enough to tell her. Her whole mindset had been changed because of her. She knew she had to speak with Annabel and thank her eventually.

"Don't let small minds convince you that your dreams are too big."

"People don't
want to hear the
truth because
they don't want
their illusions
destroyed."

Friedrich Nietzsche

"You can't convince anyone of anything, you can only give them the right information so they can convince themselves."

Eban Pagan

CHAPTER 12

SAYING GOODBYE

Many years went by and Shereen had finally saved enough to build the house. In her time, she had found a small number of Skims, including her husband and children, willing to help her build the house but not nearly enough.

Before Shereen left the house, she went to see Annabel.

Shereen: *"Hi Annabel, I've been looking for you for weeks, where have you been? I need to talk to you."*

Annabel: *"Oh, I've been on holiday Shereen. I have a lot more time and money to do the things I love since I don't pay rent as you know. What did you want to talk about?"* **Annabel asked.**

Shereen: *"Annabel you have been a great friend to me, but I have decided to build my own house. I want my family and other Skims to live rent-free too. I want us to have more time and money so that we can travel when we want to just like you do. This can only happen if I build my own house. I just wanted to use this opportunity to say thank you for everything and to say goodbye."*

Annabel: *"Wow, that's a big step Shereen. What is your vision?"*

Shereen paused for a moment then excitedly responded.

Shereen: *"I will have a massive house, Annabel. I will have schools that will teach things to the children which will encourage them to want to grow the house and invest. We will learn about our history and not only the history of the Smiths. Our history will empower us. I will make food like what my grandmother would talk about which will be better for our development and I would also love to have a bank so that we can get money to expand the house rather* *than spending it on rent and in the Smiths shops all the time. The rent money only grows the Smiths house currently Annabel. If we have our own shops, we can spend in our house, which will create money for our house, which will grow the rooms in our house and help more of our people. We will have professionals, doctors, lawyers, teachers, trainers, cooks, entrepreneurs and some of the best sports stars and entertainers. Then, because we will support each other, it will keep the money in the house and make it grow faster, just like your house did. There will be more Skims with the good jobs in my house as only a few of us get the best jobs in your house currently. We are usually chosen for many of the worst jobs first in your house."*

Annabel: *"I must say Shereen, it sounds amazing and I wish you well. Can we still be friends?*

Shereen: *"Of course, Annabel and you can come and visit my house anytime."*

"The road to
a friends
house is
never a long
one".

"Things are never quite as scary when you have a bestfriend".

CHAPTER 13

THE BUILD

So Shereen, her family and a small number of other skims, set out to build a house of their own.

It took a long time, and it was hard work but Shereen designed the house just how she wanted it.

The house had a school, a bank and several restaurants attached to it with the most amazing food. Shereen was so happy.

She wished that she could have found other people to help her build her house sooner and that she did not have to be such an elderly lady to experience the finished house. But she was happier that her children, grandchildren, great-grandchildren and generations to come would have a much better life due to the hard work she put in.

As Shereen finally put her key through the door of the house, she smiled with extreme happiness and let out a sigh of relief because although it was hard work, she had finally reached her goal of living in a house- RENT FREE and knew the sky was the limit from this point forward.

THE END

"Whatever good things we build end up building us."

Jim Rohn

"The man on top of the mountain didn't fall there."

ADDITIONAL READING

When writing this book, the idea was to create a simple story that would be able to depict a larger meaning and hopefully a call to action.

It was purposely written in a simplistic way to ensure people of all ages could understand it, read it quickly and relate to different parts of the book with their own experiences.

The following points refer to some of the concepts that were addressed in the book and some of the tips that the author has learned over the years which have helped her. These points were also recommended by other people when researching the book. Hopefully, these points will enable you to also build, manage and maintain your own houses.

TOP TIPS FOR BUILDING YOUR HOUSE

1. KNOWING THAT EDUCATION IS KEY

We often confused education solely with what we are taught in school, but education is much bigger than this and although its cliché, knowledge is power.

It is important to practice continuous learning to be able to create more options and opportunities to build your house.

What is recommended?

To play the game by following the school curriculum but to always educate yourself away from this too. Reading as much as possible to develop your mind and learning about things that are not taught in school.

To challenge and research anything that seems too bias, to get a balanced view of things that are being taught.

To always understand that learning never stops and that there is always more to know.

To learn about your history. If you understand the past, it will give you a better insight into why things you see, and experience are happening today.

"If you are not
willing to learn, no
one can help you.
If you are willing
to learn, no one
can stop you."

2. LOOKING AFTER YOUR HEALTH

(Mental health, physical, spiritual health, and your diet)

There is always a lot of emphasis on our physical health and our diet, but often many of us underestimate the importance of maintaining our mental health until something triggers us to do so. All health areas are as important as each other and should be given time and attention to be maintained.

What is recommended?

To schedule alone time for regular meditation and/or prayer.

To attend spiritual establishments or to create opportunities to be around likeminded people with common goals. Find your tribe.

To visit gyms or do regular exercise to keep your body fit and healthy.

To research food and to keep your diet clean, ensuring that what you are eating is the most suitable for you.

To practice intermittent fasting to help to re-build your cells and to rid the body of excess waste.

To think about what you are exposing yourself to. The people you interact with, the things that you watch and listen to, the books that you read, the social media pages that you follow.

How do they make you feel? These have an impact on your wellbeing and your mental/ physical health.

Understand that all areas of health E.g. diet, mental health and physical health are linked together. Research this.

"Health isn't just about what you eat, it's about what you are thinking and feeling too."

3. CHOOSING EMPLOYMENT WISELY

We are only exposed to a selection of career options when we are at school. Whether we realise it or not, this often limits our thinking in two ways.

1. It limits what we believe is possible for ourselves career-wise.

2. It determines the reasons that we want to go down a specific career path. Many people leave school with money as the main motivator when it comes to working, and as such, look for careers with the best pay cheques instead of thinking about what they are passionate about or enjoy doing. When thinking of employment, money should never be the only driver.

What is recommended?

To work to learn skills that can be used to move you into something better or to build something bigger but not just for money.

If you are working-ask yourself, what is this teaching me? How am I developing? Why do I do what I do? What is my next step from here?

Ensure that where ever you work and whatever you do, is either bringing you closer to a larger goal, is being done for enjoyment or is embracing one or more of your core values. Working alone should never be the only thing you are doing to build your house. Your families cannot inherit your job.

“Work to learn, don’t work for money.”

Robert Kiyosaki

4. UNDERSTANDING MONEY

To build your house, it is often necessary to have more than one income stream and to make good use of the money you have. It is recorded that most financially successful people have an average of seven individual income streams. Many of these are money they do not physically work for. Replacing your working income should always be a goal if you are trading in your time for money.

What is recommended?

To gain an understanding of how money works and how to make it grow.

To find out about how the credit score system works, to understand what your score is and to understand how to influence this. You will often need a good credit score to get access to money and some of the best investments, if you don't have cash.

Understand how the banks make money and how to best make money work for you.

Research residual and passive income and read books on money. Understand the difference between assets and liabilities and how to create wealth.

"Money speaks sense in a language all nations understand"

Aphra Behn

5. SELF-DEVELOPMENT

It is important to keep improving yourself. It is often said that, if you are not growing, then you are dying. Find ways to keep growing and always have something you are working towards.

What is recommended?

To regularly ask yourself questions about how you can be improving yourself and others.

Many successful people have mentors and coaches who help them to move forward and set goals.

Listening to motivation videos, reading self-development books and listen to audiobooks is also common. If there is a specific goal you are trying to achieve, consider looking into getting a mentor or coach to support.

"Knowing others is intelligence, knowing yourself is true wisdom. Mastering others is strength, mastering yourself is power."

Lao Tzu

6. GROWING YOUR NETWORK

(Your network is your net worth.)

Many opportunities that will come your way throughout life involve not only *what* you know, but also who you know too. For this reason, always embrace opportunities to network with others.

What is recommended?

Finding time to meet likeminded people by attending events for areas that you are passionate about.

Travel if possible, to understand different countries, different cultures and to meet people that are different from what you may be used to.

Guard your reputation and act with integrity. When it comes to building and maintaining relationships, trust and respect go a very long way. Stay true to your values and stay away from those who don’t respect them.

Move out of your comfort zone. Aim to understand and collaborate with other people whenever possible.

Ensure that your immediate network is positive, motivating and encouraging. If it isn’t, then find a new network.

"The time to build a network is always before you need one."

Douglas Conant

7. HAVE AN ATTITUDE OF GRATITUDE

Being thankful for what you already have, is a sure way to get more of it. There is always something to be thankful for.

What is recommended?

To always be thankful for the journey God has put you on and the things that you have learnt on the way.

To always find something to be grateful for even when you are going through challenging times. There is always something. Remember that nothing in natures blooms all year round and challenges are often necessary.

Having regular reflection time to think about your blessings and understanding that you are always being prepared for something greater, even when it may not feel that way.

"It's not happiness that brings us gratitude, it's gratitude that brings us happiness."

8. BEING MINDFUL OF WORDS

People often underestimate the power of words but studies such as Dr. Emoto's rice and water experiment is just one way to show the power words can have on us. What we say to ourselves and others is key. When you use words, aim to use them to uplift others and always speak to yourself with love.

What is recommended?

To research the significance of words. To understand that words have power and that you can speak (& think) things into existence.

To use positive, confident words as often as possible.

To be mindful of how you speak to yourself and others.

Create positive affirmations to help you attract the things you want.

Write these down or record them and repeat these often.

Your subconscious mind will start to pay attention.

Read about Dr. Emoto and the rice and water experiment for an insight on the power of words and their vibration.

"Words can
inspire and
words can
destroy - choose
yours well."

Robin Sharma

9. GOAL SETTING

To achieve the most out of life and to not just let life happen to you, it is important to set goals. What do you want out of this thing called life, if you had the choice?

What is recommended?

To be clear about what you want. Ask yourself regularly what you want and write it down. Set annual, monthly or weekly goals with small steps to get you started.

Set yourself long term goals that your smaller goals should feed into. Ensure each action step you take will bring you closer to one of your goals or core values.

Before making any major decisions, get into the habit of asking yourself "Does this support the life, I am trying to create?"

Keep the faith if things don't go to plan and congratulate yourself for the many times they will go to plan.

Regularly ask yourself: Where am I? Where do I want to be? How am I going to get there?

"If you don't know where you are going, any road will get you there."

Alice in Wonderland

10. GIVING BACK TO OTHERS

There was once a time when you didn't know some of the things that have helped to shape you today. When you learn something that can help others or even when you have something that can offer support to someone else, it's important to use it to help those people. This is a sure way to help the house grow faster.

What is recommended?

To share the knowledge, you have learned along the way with other people. To educate younger people to share what you know, especially if they are only being taught in the school system. Mentoring is a great tool to use for this.

Start discussions with friends and family to create a change in mindset and alternative ways to think about things.

To put your ego aside when it comes to helping others. It is nice to know the most or to have the best, but it is equally as rewarding to put others in a better position too.

Always remember those people who have helped you on your path in whatever capacity they did it.

Where possible, always support others in their business and charities. Be that person who always offers encouragement and assistance to others. You don't know the difference the small things can make.

"If you are lucky enough to do well, it is your responsibility to send the elevator back down."

11. NURTURING RELATIONSHIPS

The richest people are those who have others to share their memories with. Give those you care about your time and treat them with importance. This includes the relationship with yourself.

What is recommended?

To find time to spend with loved ones and people who are important to you. To make time to smile regularly. To spend time with family and likeminded friends.

To embrace the work hard, play hard motto to ensure you are enjoying your life.

To have an honest relationship with yourself and to ensure you find time to replenish your energy, in whatever form that takes for you. To have some alone time when needed, where possible.

"You don't
choose your
family, they are
God's gift to
you, as you are
to them."

Douglas Tutu

ACKNOWLEDGMENTS

I would like to thank the person who gave me the idea to write this book. We once discussed our ideas of success and this story was used as an analogy to challenge the agenda of our education system, the government, the banks and western society.

I would also like to thank God for keeping me positive and optimistic and with a hunger to motivate and provide positive change.

My individual acknowledgements go to:

Glenneca Palmer: Who helped me shape the book. For giving me ideas and feedback, which contributed to additional chapters being written. Thank you so much for your creativity.

Dominic Stewart and Cecil Quartey: For proof reading, providing ideas and consistently motivating me to turn what was planned to be a short personal story into a printed book. Thank you.

David Amuno: For proof reading, editing, providing all of the inside page graphics and feedback on the cover design. Thank you for the support.

Finally, to my family and friends who have had to listen to me repeatedly using these analogies to try and change the mindset of people around me.

I love you all and hope you enjoyed the book.

Thank you for reading

Printed in Poland
by Amazon Fulfillment
Poland Sp. z o.o., Wrocław

60650651R00096